Barty's Scarf

KU-311-398

CAVAN COUNTY LIBRARY
ACC. No. C88144
CLASS No. J 0-4
INVOICE NO. 4220
PRICE £4.99

for Jenny

Text and illustration copyright © Sally Chambers, 1998

All rights reserved. No part of this publication may be reproduced,
stored in a retrieval system, or transmitted, in any form or by any
means electronic, mechanical, photocopying or otherwise,
without prior permission of the copyright owner.

The right of Sally Chambers to be recognised as Author
of this work has been asserted by her in accordance with
the Copyright, Designs and Patents Act, 1988.

Designed by Louise Millar

Printed and bound in Belgium by Proost
for the publishers, Piccadilly Press Ltd,
5 Castle Road, London NW1 8PR

ISBNs: 1 85340 506 X (hardback)
1 85340 501 9 (paperback)

A catalogue record of this book is available from the British Library

Sally Chambers lives in Hayes, Kent.
Since graduating from the University of Brighton
she has illustrated a number of children's books,
including PEDRO for Piccadilly Press.
This is her first picture book for Piccadilly Press.

Reprinted 1998

Barty's Scarf

Sally Chambers

Piccadilly Press • London

Barty loved his woolly pink and
blue scarf which Granny had
knitted him for Christmas.
He never took it off.

CAVAN COUNTY LIBRARY

Barty's father was worried.
"How do you expect to get a counting job
jumping over fences wearing that scarf?
You'll trip up all the time."

Barty's teacher was worried.
"I can't hear if you are baa-ing properly,
when you've got that thing
slung round your neck."

Even Barty's mother was worried. "Now that the weather is getting warmer, it's very unhealthy for you to be wearing that scarf."

But Barty ignored them.
He did everything in his scarf. He played in it.

He ate in it.

He bathed in it.

And he even slept in it.

Everyone was very worried.

Some even laughed and made fun of him.

But then one day everything changed . . .

Barty was resting after playing hide and seek with the other sheep.

Suddenly he heard a faint bleating noise.

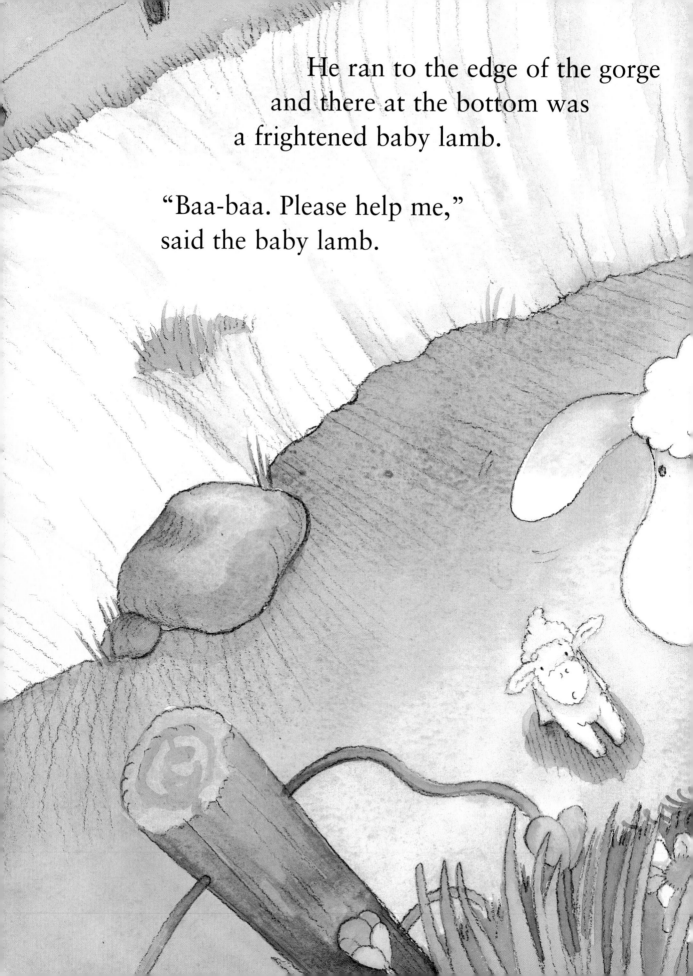

He ran to the edge of the gorge
and there at the bottom was
a frightened baby lamb.

"Baa-baa. Please help me,"
said the baby lamb.

Barty ran to get
the other sheep.

They tried to rescue the
lamb with a branch.

But he couldn't reach it.

They built a ladder for the baby lamb to climb up.

But he wouldn't climb it.

They linked legs and dangled over the edge. But they couldn't reach him.

The baby lamb was too frightened to move.

Then Barty had an idea . . .

Barty took off his scarf,
tied a big knot in it to make a loop
and lowered it into the gorge.

The baby lamb climbed inside.
The other sheep held on tight.
"Pull," said Barty. "Pull."

Everyone was so overjoyed.
The other sheep lifted Barty high in the air.
He was a hero.

The mayor gave him a trophy.
Everyone was happy for Barty.
No one ever teased him about
his wonderful scarf ever again.

CAVAN COUNTY LIBRARY

Top Sheep

But then Barty received another present.